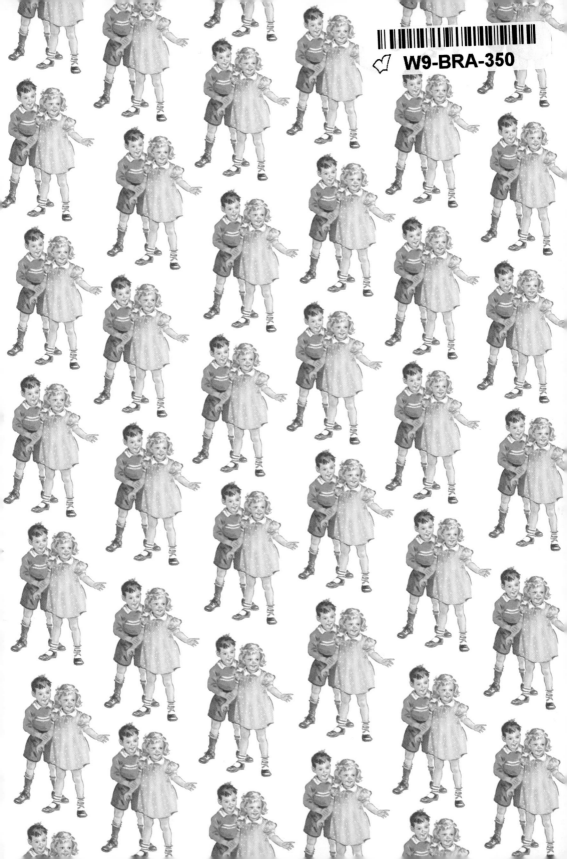

This Book Belongs to

_____

Learn to Read with
Dick and Jane

PENGUIN YOUNG READERS
AN IMPRINT OF PENGUIN RANDOM HOUSE

PENGUIN YOUNG READERS
An Imprint of Penguin Random House LLC

ISBN 9781101951040   10   9   8   7   6   5   4   3   2   1

Learn to Read with
Dick and Jane

Dick and Jane
Jump and Run

Penguin Young Readers
An Imprint of Penguin Random House LLC.

Chapters

Chapter 1
Puff

Jump, Puff.

Jump, jump, jump.

Jump, Puff, jump.

Run, Puff.

Run, Puff, run.

Run, run, run.

Jump, jump, jump.

Oh, Puff.

Oh, oh, oh.

Funny, funny Puff.

Chapter 2
Spot

Come, come.

Come, Spot, come.

Run, run, run.

Jump, Spot.

Jump, jump.

Jump, Spot, jump.

Oh, Spot.

Oh, oh, oh.

Funny, funny Spot.

Chapter 3
Jump and Play

Sally said, "Oh, look.

Mother can jump.

Mother can jump and play."

Dick said, "Jump, Father.

You can jump.

You can jump and play."

"Look, Mother," said Sally.

"See Father jump.

See Father jump and play.

Big, big Father is funny."

Jane said, "Oh, Father.

You can not jump and play.

Spot can not jump and play."

Dick said, "Oh, see Puff.

Puff can jump.

Puff can jump and play."

Chapter 4
Run and Help

Run, Jane.

Help Mother.

Run, Jane, run.

Help Mother work.

Come, Sally, come.

Come and help.

Come and help Mother.

Run, run, run.

Look, Sally, look.

See Spot work.

Funny, funny Spot.

Oh, oh, oh.

Spot can help Mother.

Chapter 5
See Puff Jump

Look, Dick.

See Puff jump.

Oh, look.

Look and see.

See Puff jump and play.

Come, Jane, come.

Come and see Puff.

See Puff jump and run.

See funny, little Puff.

Oh, oh, oh.

See little Puff run.

Oh, see Puff.

Funny, little Puff.

Chapter 6
Spot and Tim and Puff

Spot can jump.

Little Puff can jump.

Look, Tim, look.

See Spot and Puff play.

Look, Tim.

See Sally jump.

See Sally jump down.

Down, down, down.

Sally can jump and play.

Oh, Puff.

See funny, little Tim.

See Tim jump down.

Down, down, down.

Tim can jump and play.

Chapter 7
Oh, See

Look, Sally, look.

Look down.

Look down, Sally.

Look down, down, down.

Look up, Sally.

Look up, up, up.

Run, Sally, run.

Run and jump.

Run and jump up.

Look, Jane.

Look and see.

Oh, see.

See funny, funny Sally.

Dick and Jane
Away We Go

Penguin Young Readers
An Imprint of Penguin Random House LLC.

Chapters

Chapter 1
Tim

Jump up, Sally.

Jump up.

Come, Sally.

Jump up.

Jump up, Tim.

Jump up.

Up, up, up.

Jump up.

Look, Dick.

See Sally and Tim.

Funny, funny Sally.

Funny, funny Tim.

Chapter 2
Tim and Spot

Go, Tim.

Go up.

Go up, Tim.

Go up, up, up.

Go, Tim.

Go down.

Go, go, go.

Go down.

Go down, down, down.

Oh, Jane.

See Spot and Tim.

See Spot run.

See funny Spot.

See funny Tim.

Chapter 3
Up, Tim

Up, Puff, up.

Come, Puff, come.

Oh, oh.

See Puff jump down.

Up, Puff, up.

Jump up, Puff.

Jump up.

See Tim.

Up, Tim, up.

Chapter 4
Run Away, Spot

"Oh, Spot," said Jane.

"You cannot play here."

Jane said,

"I can make a house."

"I can make a little house,"

said Jane.

"Down comes my house,"

said Jane.

"Down it comes.

Run away, Spot.

You cannot play here."

Chapter 5
Down It Comes

Dick said, "I can make a house.

A big house for two boats.

A house for the yellow boat.

And for the blue boat.

See my big house."

Jane said, "I can make a house.

A big house for three cars.

Red and blue and yellow cars."

Sally said, "I can make a house.

A little house for Tim.

Here is my house for Tim.

Tim is in it.

Tim can play in it.

Oh, oh, oh.

Tim looks funny in the house."

"See my house," said Dick.

"Down it comes."

"See my house," said Jane.

"Down, down it comes."

"Oh, oh, oh," said Sally.

"Down comes my little house.

Run away, Puff.

Run away, Spot.

You cannot play here."

Chapter 6
Away We Go

Sally said, "Away we go.

Away we go in the car.

Mother and Father.

Dick and Jane.

Sally and Tim."

Dick said, "Spot is not here.

Puff is not here."

Dick said, "I see something.

Look down, Jane.

Look down and see something.

It is funny.

Can you see it?"

"Oh, oh," said Jane.

"Here is Spot."

"Come in, Spot," said Jane.

"You can go in the car."

"Away we go," said Sally.

"Away we go in the car.

Mother and Father.

Dick and Jane.

Sally and Tim and Spot.

Away we go in the big, big car."

Chapter 7
See It Go

Jane said, "Look, look.

I see a big yellow car.

See the yellow car go."

Sally said, "I see it.

I see the big yellow car.

I want to go away in it.

I want to go away, away."

Dick said, "Look up, Sally.

You can see something.

It is red and yellow.

It can go up, up, up.

It can go away."

Sally said, "I want to go up.

I want to go up in it.

I want to go up, up, up.

I want to go up and away."

"Look, Sally," said Dick.

"Here is Father in a boat.

You can go away in it."

"Jump in, jump in," said Father.

"Jump in the big blue boat."

"We can go," said Sally.

"We can go away in the boat.

Away in a big blue boat."

Dick and Jane
Go, Go, Go

Penguin Young Readers
An Imprint of Penguin Random House LLC.

Chapters

Chapter 1
Go, Go, Go

Come, Spot.

Come and go.

Jump, jump.

Jump up, Spot.

Jump up.

Oh, Jane.

Look and see.

See Sally go.

See Tim go.

See Spot and Puff go.

Oh, Dick.

Look and see.

See Spot jump down.

See Puff jump down.

Down, down, down.

Oh, oh, oh.

Chapter 2
Come

Come, Sally.

Come, come.

Oh, Sally.

Come, come.

Come, Sally, come.

Oh, see.

See Sally go.

Go, Sally, go.

Go, go, go.

Chapter 3
See Jane Go

Oh, Sally.

See Jane go down.

Down, down, down.

See Jane go down.

Look, Jane.

Look, look.

Oh, look.

Look, Tim, look.

Oh, look.

See funny, funny Jane.

See funny Jane go.

Chapter 4
Sally and Mother

Sally said, "Oh, see.

See Mother go.

Come, Dick.

Come, Jane.

Come and go."

Jane said, "Oh, Dick.

See Sally and Tim.

Oh, oh, oh.

See Baby Sally go.

Go, Dick, go."

Sally said, "Oh, Mother.

See Dick go down.

See Jane go down.

Funny, funny Dick and Jane."

Chapter 5
The Boats Go

Oh, Dick.

The blue boat can go.

The yellow boat can go.

My little, red car can go.

Look, look.

See my red car go.

91

Oh, oh.

See my red car.

See my red car go down.

Down, down, down.

Oh, Dick.

Help, help.

My little, red car is down.

Up, up, up.

Up comes the little, red car.

See Dick help.

See the little, red car come up.

Up, up, up.

The little, red car is up.

Chapter 6
The Big, Red Boat

Come, Baby Sally.

Come and see Father work.

See Father make boats.

The little boat is my boat.

I can make my boat blue.

See my little, blue boat.

Look, Sally, look.

See my big boat.

I can make my boat red.

Look, Sally.

See my boat.

See my big, red boat.

Oh, look, look.

See Puff jump.

See my boat go down.

Oh, look.

My boat is yellow.

Dick and Jane
Something Funny

Penguin Young Readers
An Imprint of Penguin Random House LLC.

Chapters

Chapter 1
Dick

Look, Dick.

Look, look.

Oh, oh.

Look, Dick.

Oh, oh.

See Dick.

Oh, see Dick.

Chapter 2
Sally

Look, Sally.

Look, look.

See Jane.

Oh, Jane.

See Sally.

See little Sally.

Little, little Sally.

Look, Jane.

See funny Sally.

Oh, oh, oh.

Funny, little Sally.

Chapter 3
Help, Help

Look, Dick.

See Spot.

Oh, see Spot.

Help, help.

Oh, Jane.

See Spot.

Oh, see Spot.

Come, Jane, come.

Help, help, help.

Look, Dick.

See Spot and Sally.

Come see Sally.

See funny, little Sally.

Chapter 4
Sally Sees Something

Come, Sally.

Come and look.

Come and see, Sally.

Funny, little Sally.

Dick, Dick.

Help, help.

I see something.

Help, help, help.

I see something.

Look, Sally.

I see something.

I see Baby Sally.

Little Baby Sally.

Look, look.

See funny Baby Sally.

Chapter 5
Something Funny

Look, Dick.

Look, look.

I see something funny.

Come and see.

Come and see Spot.

Oh, Jane.

I see something funny.

Come, Jane, come.

See Spot and Baby Sally.

Come and help.

Look, Dick.

See Jane help Spot.

Oh, see something funny.

See little Spot.

Funny, little Spot.

Chapter 6
Make Something Funny

Oh, Dick, look.

I can make Tim and Puff.

Tim is yellow.

Puff is red.

Make something, Dick.

Make something yellow.

Make something blue.

I can make something blue.

I can make blue cars.

I can make blue boats.

See my cars and boats.

See the funny, blue boat.

See the funny, blue car.

Look, Jane, look.

Up go the boats.

Up go the cars.

Up, up go Tim and Puff.

Down come the boats.

Down come the cars.

Down comes Tim.

Down comes Puff.

Down,

down,

down.

Dick and Jane
We Look

Penguin Young Readers
An Imprint of Penguin Random House LLC.

Chapters

Chapter 1
Look

Look, look.

Oh, oh, oh.

Oh, oh.

Oh, look.

Chapter 2
Jane

Oh, Jane.

Look, Jane, look.

Look, look.

Oh, look.

See Jane.

See, see.

See Jane.

Oh, see Jane.

Chapter 3
Dick

Look, Jane.

Look, look.

See Dick.

See, see.

Oh, see.

See Dick.

Oh, see Dick.

Oh, oh, oh.

Funny, funny Dick.

Chapter 4
Sally

Look, Dick.

Look, Jane.

See Sally.

Oh, oh, oh.

Oh, Dick.

See Sally.

Look, Jane.

Look, Dick.

See funny Sally.

Funny, funny Sally.

Chapter 5
Big and Little

Come, come.

Come and see.

See Father and Mother.

Father is big.

Mother is little.

Look, Father.

Dick is big.

Sally is little.

Big, big Dick.

Little Baby Sally.

Oh, look, Jane.

Look, Dick, look.

Sally is big.

Tim is little.

Big, big Sally.

Little Baby Tim.

Chapter 6
The Funny Baby

Come down, Dick.

Come and see.

See the big, big mother.

See the funny little baby.

Puff is my baby.

Puff is my funny little baby.

I see the big mother.

I see the little baby.

Look, Jane.

See the big father.

Look, Dick, look.

See something funny.

See my baby jump.

See my baby run.

Oh, oh, oh.

Chapter 7
Something Blue

Oh, Jane, I see something.

I see something blue.

Come and see Mother work.

Mother can make something.

Something blue.

Look, Mother, look.

I can work.

I can make something.

I can make something yellow.

Look, look.

See something yellow.

Oh, Jane, I can work.

I can make something blue.

I can make something yellow.

Oh, see my funny Tim.

Little Tim is yellow.

Baby Sally is blue.

Dick and Jane
We Play

Penguin Young Readers
An Imprint of Penguin Random House LLC.

Chapters

Chapter 1
Play

Oh, Father.

See funny Dick.

Dick can play.

Oh, Mother.

Oh, Father.

Jane can play.

Sally can play.

Oh, Father.

See Spot.

Funny, funny Spot.

Spot can play.

Chapter 2

See Dick Play

Look, Jane.

Look, look.

Look and see.

See Father play.

See Dick play.

Look, Mother.

Look, Mother, look.

See Father.

See Father and Dick.

Oh, Mother.

See Spot.

Look, Mother, look.

Spot can help Dick.

Chapter 3

Funny Spot

Come, Spot.

Come, come.

Play, Spot.

Play, play.

Go, Spot.

Go, go.

Spot can play.

Dick can play.

Oh, oh.

Funny, funny Spot.

Chapter 4

See Spot Play

See Jane jump.

Jump, jump.

See Spot jump.

Jump, jump.

Oh, Dick.

Oh, Jane.

See Spot.

Funny, funny Spot.

Spot can play.

Chapter 5
Funny Father

"Come, Jane," said Father.

"Come and play ball.

Come and play."

"I can help you play ball,"

said Father.

"I can help."

"Come, Father," said Jane.

"Come and play ball.

Come and play."

Oh, funny, funny Father.

Chapter 6

Play Ball

"Come, Jane," said Father.

"Come and play ball.

Come and play."

"Oh," said Jane.

"See the red ball go.

See it go up, up, up.

Run, Dick, run."

"Oh, oh," said Dick.

"Where is my ball?

I can not find it.

Come here, Jane.

Run and help me.

Help me find my red ball."

"I can help you," said Jane.

"We can find the red ball."

Dick said, "I see it.

I see my red ball.

Look, Father.

See where it is.

Come and help me."

Jane said, "Oh, Dick.

Spot can help you.

Spot can find the ball."

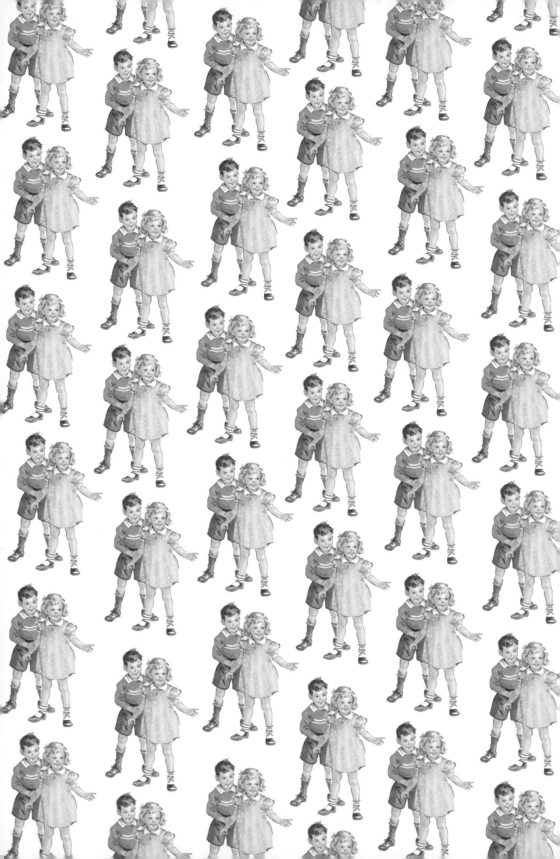